Mockingbird

Mockingbird

ALLAN AHLBERG

ILLUSTRATED BY
PAUL HOWARD

WALKER BOOKS
AND SUBSIDIARIES
LONDON • BOSTON • SYDNEY

Rhymes
Babies

Hush little baby,
   don't say a word,

Mama's gonna buy you ...

a Mockingbird.

If that Mockingbird won't sing,
Papa's gonna buy you ...

a garden swing.

If that garden swing gets stuck,
Polly's gonna buy you ...

a pedal truck.

If that pedal truck tips over,

Rosie's gonna buy you ...

a dog named Rover.

If that dog named Rover runs away,

Granny's gonna chase him ...

if it takes all day!

If it takes all day and starts to ...

rain,

Mama's gonna hurry you home again.

She'll wipe your face and dry your hair,

sit you up in your own high chair,

tie your bib and~for goodness' sake~

Papa's gone and baked you ...

a birthday cake.

Tired little baby, sleepy head,

   Mama's gonna tuck you in your bed.

Close your eyes, don't say a word,

maybe have a dream ...

of a Mockingbird.

For Collette and Kieran
– P.H.

First published 1998 by Walker Books Ltd, 87 Vauxhall Walk, London SE11 5HJ

2 4 6 8 10 9 7 5 3 1

Text © 1998 Allan Ahlberg Illustrations © 1998 Paul Howard

This book has been typeset in Usherwood book

Printed in Belgium

British Library Cataloguing in Publication Data
A catalogue record for this book is available from the British Library.

ISBN 0-7445-5574-4